Tales from the Canyons of the Damned

PRESENTED BY USA TODAY BESTSELLING AUTHOR
DANIEL ARTHUR SMITH

Tales from the Canyons of the Damned 33

All rights reserved Holt Smith ltd

Collection Copyright © 2019 by Daniel Arthur Smith

Auntie_lena314 by Molly Thynes. Copyright © 2018 Molly Thynes. Used by permission of the author.

A Wonder Made of Skulls by Barry Charman. Copyright © 2018 Barry Charman. Used by permission of the author.

Masks by Jason LaVelle. Copyright © 2018 Jason LaVelle. Used by permission of the author.

Off-World Kick Murder Squad VI by Daniel Arthur Smith. Copyright © 2019 Daniel Arthur Smith. Used by permission of the author.

First Edition

Special thanks to editor Jessica West

ISBN: 978-1-946777-88-1

Cover By Daniel Arthur Smith

Horror Fiction from Holt Smith ltd
Agroland
Tower
Attack of the Kung Fu Mummies

For Susan, Tristan, & Oliver, as all things are.

Auntie_lena314
Molly Thynes

THERE USED TO BE a video channel online. It was called Auntie_lena314. The videos have long since been taken down and even the channel as a whole was blocked.

She posted her first video on May 27th. For the first ten seconds, you saw just a teenage girl with sun bleached hair in a pink cardigan fiddling with the webcam, showing just how inexperienced she was with creating web videos.

"Hello, world! My name is Auntie Lena," she said as she took a seat in the desk chair.

She told the viewers that this wasn't going to be a video channel about boy bands or makeup. Her voice squealing, she told everyone how her nephew, Henry, had just been born yesterday. She created this channel to document the earliest moments of his life.

She was especially excited because her sister, Nan, was going to be moving back home with Henry. She wouldn't be able to keep a baby in the dorms.

"Nan's not too thrilled about moving back home, but at least it's rent-free and she'll have a place to live."

Auntie Lena promised to post a video every few days. She talked about how adorable her nephew was, how she was sure she saw him smile at her. She would film little Henry in the different outfits that relatives sent, chubby and pink with a few strands of almost-red hair. In some of the videos, she appears with dark circles under her eyes, saying little Henry had kept her up all night crying, or he was struggling with a particularly bad bout of colic. But for the most part, they stayed boring little mundane videos in Nan's little room, and the views never climbed above thirty.

Then, on June 13th, she posted a video where she was fidgeting, biting her lip, her hands clenching the seat of her chair. She told the viewers about her sister, Nan. She was refusing to change him or feed him, and for the last three days, she hadn't changed her clothes or brushed her hair.

"I've been doing a lot of reading online," Auntie Lena said, her eyes avoiding the camera. "I think Nan might have postpartum depression. I might not be putting up a new video for a few days, because I want to do some more reading about this."

But on June 16th, things seemed to be getting worse. Auntie Lena started the video by thanking all her viewers for the articles they had sent on postpartum depression.

"But Nan's been getting worse," Auntie Lena said, holding the camera in front of her face as she walked down the hallway.

When Auntie Lena turned the camera around, she was standing in the doorway to Nan's bedroom. In the center of the room, Nan stood with slumped shoulders, dressed in wrinkled, damp pajamas, her hair stringy and oily. As

Auntie Lena moved closer to her sister, you could see that Nan was standing over the baby's bassinette.

"Nan?" Auntie Lena asked as she moved to film her sister's face. "Nan, will you say something to me?"

As Nan's face came into profile, you could just make out her lips moving as she looked down at her baby. If you had your headphones on and the volume turned all the way up, you could just barely hear Nan's words.

"Not mine...he's not my baby...how does no one else notice?"

Auntie Lena spent almost a minute trying to get her sister's attention, even shoving the camera right into her sister's face, but Nan didn't so much as look away or tell her sister to leave her alone. Eventually, Auntie Lena gave up and returned to her room. She set the camera back on top of the computer and settled into her chair once again.

"She's been like this for days. I don't mean just the not taking care of herself or Henry. She's saying all these weird things about how Henry's not her baby. I know that women with postpartum depression say they feel a disconnect from their babies, but this just seems...off."

Reaching off to the side, Auntie Lena grabbed a few sheets of printed paper.

"One of the things I came across in these articles is this thing called postpartum psychosis. Maybe that's what happening, but I don't know. Mom and Dad are trying to get Nan in to see a doctor. I hope it happens soon."

Then, on June 18th, anyone who was awake in the middle of the night saw a...disturbing new upload to Auntie Lena's channel. The video opened to pitch black with Auntie Lena fumbling with the camera, as though she was just waking up and trying to remember how to turn it on.

"Do you hear that?"

In the dark frame, you could just make out the outline of Auntie Lena's face, but this wasn't a camera with a night vision function, so pretty much all you had to go on was the audio. You could hear the *rustle rustle* as Auntie Lena kicked off the sheets and climbed out of bed, the soft sound of her bare feet as she ventured out into the hallway.

Finally, you were able to see some light coming from the crack under a door.

"Nan? Are you up?"

Auntie Lena opened the door and held up the camera to show Nan once again standing over Henry's bassinette. In one hand, she was gripping tight to a box of matches. Then the camera picked up a bright flash of light as Nan struck a match and dangled it over the bassinette.

"DAD!" Auntie Lena shrieked as she leaned out into the hallway. From the furthest door down, a silver-haired man bolted out into the hall, nearly crashing into Auntie Lena.

"Nan, don't!"

Their father rushed into the room, pushing Nan away from the baby, grabbing tight around her wrist until his knuckles turned white. Nan lost her grip on the match, sending it flying towards the curtains. Flames raced along the bottom hem, and climbed upward towards the ceiling.

In the struggle, Auntie Lena rushed into the bathroom, pulling a bucket from under the sink. As she filled it with water, you could hear Nan scream from the other room. "It has to die! It has to be burned!"

Running back to the room, she tossed the camera onto the bed. The frame went sideways, but showed Auntie Lena splashing water onto the fire while Nan struggled with everything she had to get away from her father, who was using the whole of his body weight to keep her pinned to the floor.

"Paul, what's happened?" a woman shouted from outside the frame.

"Janet, call 911!"

Auntie Lena managed to put out the fire and looked back to toward the bed, as though she had just remembered she had left the camera running. Shooting past her father and sister, she reached for the camera and the video came to an end.

Why she even posted a video like that, none of her viewers were able to figure out. The host site did have a function where you could stream live video from your camera directly to the site, so Auntie Lena probably had no idea what she was about to walk into. People were trading different theories back and forth in the comment section of her other videos almost immediately after it happened.

On June 19th, Auntie Lena appeared on camera, white as a bedsheet.

"Nan's gone."

After Auntie Lena had cut off the video footage, the police came to the house. Even in the presence of men with guns, Nan refused to stop fighting or insisting that her baby had to die. It took both of them to force Nan out of the room and out of the house.

"We just got an update this morning."

Nan was being transferred from the jail to a psychiatric hospital. They were trying a bunch of different medications, but Nan would be staying there until the County Attorney decided what to do with her.

On June 25th, little Henry appeared for the first time on camera. Auntie Lena explained that with Nan away, she had to step up and take over a lot of the care of her nephew.

"At least it's summer vacation. Health class was right when they said high school kids aren't meant to raise children."

You see, little Henry was not an easy baby to take care of. He would cry at all hours of the night, and for most of the daytime hours too. He had been difficult to breastfeed, but he wasn't taking to the bottle any better. His skin was loose and it didn't have that baby-soft feel that people went on and on about, and it even seemed to be taking on a blueish grey color. And Auntie Lena was terrified that the baby was going to starve.

On some level, the more Auntie Lena talked about Henry, the easier it was to see how her sister could have lost her mind taking care of him.

On June 27th, Lena appeared on camera with dark circles under her eyes. She was holding her head in her hand, twisting her hair around her fingers.

"I'm wondering...is it possible for babies to go insane? Because I think that's what's happening to Henry."

She said Henry was becoming much more than just a fussy baby. He still cried as much as ever, but the cries themselves had begun taking on an entirely different, more distressing tone. Not the cry of a baby, but...

Auntie Lena listed off everything that reminded her more of Henry's cries. Someone who had had their hand slammed in the door, someone who had a cigar put out on their thigh, a cat having its tail sawed off. The cries of someone who suffered agonizing pain just from existing.

Auntie Lena struggled to detail everything that was happening. She was slumped in her chair, struggling to keep eye contact with the camera. Whenever she did manage to look her viewers in the eyes, you could see the dull luster both her eyes and her skin were taking on.

"What he needs right now is his mom, but Nan isn't going to be coming back for a long time."

For several days, no new videos were posted on Auntie Lena's channel. Instead, she set up a live video feed right in front of Henry's bassinet. On the first night, Auntie Lena got in front of the camera and told the viewers she was going to learn what was happening at night once and for all.

For three nights, nothing happened. Like Auntie Lena said, Henry would cry at all hours of the night. But then on the fourth night, everyone up at three in the morning got to see one of the 'crazy fits' Auntie Lena was talking about. From the slanted angle, you watched Henry shake, just a little bit, then begin screaming the most ungodly scream. It didn't stop there. The baby began convulsing, his head bending backwards, pushing his little chest upward.

Finally, it all ended with a fit so violent, Henry propelled himself out of the bassinet, where he just laid limp and crying until Auntie Lena stumbled into the scene.

After the live feed, Auntie Lena didn't post anything for over a week. And with the view count on her videos skyrocketing, the comments section began piling up.

Make another video, crazy girl.

Fakey fake fake.

When do we get to see the demon baby again?

Then, on July 1st, Auntie Lena appeared on camera once again. For the first several seconds of the video, Auntie Lena did not look at the camera. Her hair was lank, stringy, and unwashed. She was still wearing her pajamas, and from the wrinkles and the stains, she had clearly been wearing them for days.

"Well, you've all seen the livestream of Henry. I've seen it too. I'm…just not sure what it was I saw."

Of course, she told her viewers, she had shown the video of what happened to her parents. Horrified, little Henry was taken straight to the doctor. Every test the tiny county clinic was capable of performing was done on Henry, each of them turning up nothing.

"The doctors actually saw the exact same tape you all saw, but even they don't know what's happening right now."

The family would have to take Henry to a larger hospital two hours away if they wanted any kind of medical answers.

On July 5th, Auntie Lena posted another video in what felt like a much more eerily quiet house. In her more recent videos, no matter how faint, you could usually make out Henry crying from somewhere in the background, or Auntie Lena's parents pacing the halls back and forth, walking him, rocking him, trying to calm him down. But today, it was just Auntie Lena, her and a book with a blue quilted cover she held in her lap as she played with the fringes along the edge.

"Mom and Dad drove Henry out to the hospital yesterday. The doctors want scans of his brain."

Auntie Lena had chosen to stay behind.

"Please don't send me any more messages. I'm not really interested in what strangers think anymore."

Auntie Lena held the quilted book up against her chest. Still bright and brand knew, the tiny details, like the bright yellow ducks or white airplanes, stood out brightly.

"Besides," she said as she opened the book, "I think I have everything I need right here."

Auntie Lena confessed that she had gone snooping through Nan's room and, shoved underneath the mattress, she found the baby book Nan had bought for Henry. Auntie Lena held the book up to the camera. It showed the first photo taken of him at the hospital, the little card that had been on his crib, his hospital bracelet, his little black ink footprints. All the cute little mementos mothers saved after their children were born.

"But here's where it starts getting strange."

She flipped three pages forward, and that's where the actual baby book ended. Instead, the next several pages were filled with writing. Lists, paragraphs, small and large letters filling up the pages from margin to margin. Between that and how Auntie Lena had found it under her sister's mattress, the thing read more like a serial killer manifesto than a baby book. People said as much in the comments.

"Nan wrote all this," Auntie Lena told her viewers. "Let me read some of it to you."

Auntie Lena opened the book. At first, Nan's writing was simply a mirror of what Auntie Lena had been recording in her videos. Henry wouldn't eat; Henry was colicky and fussy. And because of it all, his skin was losing its softness, and his fine little strands of hair were turning sticky and clumping together.

Then came an entry about a horrific nightmare Nan had one night.

"The entire house was on fire. Somehow, I was managing to avoid all the flames, but then I saw Lena stagger from around the corner, completely engulfed. Lena ran for Henry's bassinet. Then she picked him up in her arms while she was still on fire, and he started to shriek as Lena's flames spread to him."

But what was truly terrifying was everything that happened after.

"Even after I woke up, the screams followed me into the waking world. But eventually I realized that the screams were coming from Henry, the sort of sounds a person could only make as the flesh was charred from their bones.

"Since that nightmare, I haven't been able to sleep at night." With all Henry's crying, he never let Nan sleep for more than a few hours at a time anyway.

So instead, Nan would stay up at night, just watching her baby and detailing everything she saw in Henry's little baby book.

She made note of every one of Henry's horrific cries, comparing each one to some horrific pain that could be inflicted on a human being, just as Auntie Lena had done when she first started detailing Henry's disturbing behaviors, before she knew her sister was doing the exact same thing.

Doctors are always so quick to write off a young, hysterical mother.

The rest of what Auntie Lena read were Nan's speculation on just what could be wrong with her baby. It started off with some fairly mundane guesses – *she wasn't feeding him enough, he had some kind of disease from birth that the doctors missed*—gradually becoming more fantastic—*he had picked up some tropical fungus from the gifts from relatives in Florida*—and horrifying—*someone was poisoning him*—on and on and on.

"Eventually, she just starts writing this same word over and over again," Auntie Lena said, finally looking up at the camera. "Changeling."

After that video, Auntie Lena became much more faithful about weekly postings; most weeks, posting two or three. But by now, Auntie Lena had chosen to go in a different creative direction with her channel. Instead of Auntie Lena sitting at her desk in her bedroom, these videos all featured Henry. Gone were the adorable, Facebook-worthy videos, and in their place was something more out of a horror movie. Henry's skin had turned a sickly yellow-grey. His face, his arms, his chest displayed all these crater-like lesions: deep, but none of them were scabbed or bleeding.

In one video, little Henry was on his stomach, laying on the floor, the camera propped up right in front of him. Henry was bawling his same jarring cry. Auntie Lena's feet paced back and forth behind him across the frame. This went on for about thirty seconds until it was just Henry alone in the shot.

And then...*crash*! A glass pitcher dropped to the floor, right in front of the baby. Shards of glass flew through the air, a few across the baby's face, slicing open his left cheek. Blood poured from the cuts, but that wasn't what people reacted to most in the video. It was Henry's silence following, the first silence the viewers had ever seen from the baby. Face still smeared with tears and snot and blood, the baby just stared out at the broken glass, completely transfixed.

That's where the video cut out.

At this point, the comment section exploded with people saying they were reporting her channel, that they were calling the police.

Auntie Lena finally addressed these comments on July 30th. For that video, she went back to her old format of her sitting in her room in front of her computer.

"I've been reading all your comments," Auntie Lena's voice was flat. "You can show these videos to the police, but they probably won't believe any of this is real. Nothing I've filmed is anything a baby should be capable of."

Auntie Lena reached for some wrinkled papers on the desk. "And that's exactly what I wanted to show all of you."

With her one free hand, Auntie Lena shifted the camera left, bringing into view the blue bassinet Henry slept in, in her bedroom.

"Nan suspected and she did her best get the proof." Now Auntie Lena reached for the same baby book she had shown her viewers before. "But I think I finally managed, with these videos, to show that there is absolutely no doubt."

Auntie Lena looked over her shoulder and pointed to the bassinet.

"Henry, the baby you've all been seeing, is not Henry."

Settling back into her seat, Auntie Lena opened the baby book and began flipping through the pages, frantic to the point where she was nearly ripping them.

"In the last parts of Nan's writing, she starts talking a lot about this thing called a changeling," she said. "Babies are taken and replaced with…spirits, demons, or just enchanted objects."

In the background, you could make out the very faintest whimpers and stirring from the bassinet. Auntie Lena ignored them.

"I'm not quite sure when it happened, Nan wasn't really clear on that, but Henry was taken and replaced by that…thing."

Auntie Lena reached over to the side of the desk and held up a stack of wrinkled computer printouts. "Everything I've read says that very often, babies who were disabled or deformed were accused of being changelings, but there are a few ways to know if your baby has truly been taken.

"They cry relentlessly and nothing can console them. Things that normally terrify babies make changelings laugh, or at the very least, stop crying for a few minutes. They are capable of physical feats that human infants are not. And as time passes, they gradually become less and less human-looking."

As if to emphasize this last point, Auntie Lena picked up the camera and carried it over to peer inside the bassinet. Henry lay inside, rasping and jerking unnaturally, like someone on the edges of death.

Auntie Lena turned the camera back to face herself. "There are ways to get rid of a changeling, and some of them even force whoever took your baby to bring it back.

"But…" Auntie Lena looked away, suddenly avoiding eye contact with the camera, "I'm ready to start taking your messages again. If any of you have heard stories about changelings, anything you wouldn't find on the Internet, please tell me. There…aren't a lot of good options I've come across so far."

It was this video that brought all the crazies out. People claiming to be paranormal investigators or cryptozoologists in their comments began listing all the gruesome ways Irish peasants would rid themselves of monsters they thought had replaced their children. That's when Auntie Lena's viewers, who had been there from the beginning, began shouting back.

What the hell do you think you're doing?!?!?!

Have you been watching this girl? She's cray-cray!!!

Stop pushing her! This girl's gonna snap! Don't give her ideas!

Then, Auntie Lena posted what would be her last video.

On July 31st, Auntie Lena set up another special livestream, opening in the family kitchen. As Auntie Lena adjusted the camera, you could see Henry lying behind her. The room was dark, lit only by the streetlamps outside and the bluer light of the moon.

"Thank you all for joining me tonight. Mom and Dad are out...again. To be honest, they really haven't been home much at all lately."

When Auntie Lena moved away from the camera, you could see a large pot on the stove, the kind people used to cook lobster.

"Well, even though it's only been a day, I've received a lot of messages from all of you. But only a few of them were about changelings. Unfortunately, with a few rare exceptions, you don't seem to know much more about changelings than I do."

In the comment section to the right of the video, all of the pervious 'experts' were notably absent. Only Auntie Lena's gathering of loyal followers were there, typing a slow trickle of messages, all repeating different variations of asking her just what was going on.

"There are a lot of ways to find out if there is a changeling in your home, but I've only found two ways of driving one out.

"One is with water, submerging the creature," Auntie Lena said, placing a lid over the large pot. "The other is with fire."

Auntie Lena turned the dial on the gas stove and blue flames shot up from the burner.

"Both are supposed to drive the changeling out of your home," she said, bending down to pick up Henry. "Tonight's going to be a very special episode, because we're going to be testing both at once."

Auntie Lena, with her back to the camera, walked towards the counter. For once, the baby's constant cries had quieted to a few soft whimpers. Auntie Lena bounced him up and down until clear strings of steam rose from up under the lid of the pot on the stove. As the rapid bubbling and busting noises of the boiling water overpowered the hissing of the gas, the comments starting coming through faster and more frantically.

Auntie Lena, what are you doing?!?!

Someone call 911!!!

How?!?! We don't know where she is!!!!!!

Does anyone know how to track the stream?

Lena!!! Don't do something you can't take back!!!!

Auntie Lena lifted the lid from the pot and looked over her shoulder, staring directly into the camera. "You've all seen what I've seen, so you know why I have to do this."

Auntie Lena maneuvered Henry away from her hip, dangling him above the boiling pot. Henry showed no awareness for his surroundings, or of what his aunt was about to do to him; he simply stared blankly out ahead of him, legs hanging limp. Then, Auntie Lena simply dropped him right into the boiling water.

Water splashed and spilled over the stove and onto the countertops, splashing onto Auntie Lena as well. But instead of screaming, like anyone else would have, Auntie Lena slammed the lid of the pot, holding it tightly in place.

The most horrible shrieks you ever heard came from within that pot, which was shaking so violently, Auntie Lena had to stand with the whole of her body weight over the lid just to keep the pot over the burner.

When it finally stopped, Auntie Lena sank to the floor. The previous comments all went dead quiet as silence overtook the kitchen. Then, Auntie Lena reached into her pocket and pulled out her cellphone.

"Hello...my nephew is dead. No, I haven't checked his pulse or done any of that. Because I know he's dead.

Because I burned him in a pot. You should send someone here."

For several moments, Auntie Lena just stared up at the ceiling. Eventually, her head tilted slowly down until her eyes stared directly into the camera.

"I told you all this was going to be a very special episode."

Finally, from outside the view of the camera, came a loud banging on the door. Auntie Lena got up from the floor and picked up the camera.

"Police! Open the door!"

"It's not locked."

The off-screen door flew open and crashed against the wall and two officers—both young men—entered the frame: Officer Regis and Officer Jamison, from the names on their badges.

"Where's the baby?"

The camera turned toward the steaming pot and showed Auntie Lena pointing towards it.

Officer Regis rushed towards the stove, with Officer Jamison right after him, even though there was no chance of saving the baby after it had been boiling for so long.

"I had to do it. We don't have a fireplace and this was the next best thing."

Officer Regis grabbed the pot off the stove with his bare hands and dumped it into the sink, the whole time shouting as the scalding metal burned his hands and the water spattered over his wrists.

Officer Jameson pulled out his flashlight to examine his partner's bright red skin.

The injured officer groaned as the water gurgled down the sink. Clearly, neither of them were listening to Auntie Lena, but still, she continued to explain herself.

"He wasn't a real baby, you see. Whatever it was, we've had it here for weeks, and I spent the whole time trying to figure out what to do with it. I don't know how long it will take to get the real baby back."

"There's no baby here."

"What?" Auntie Lena shrieked, running to the sink, taking the camera with her. Inside, instead of the horror there should have been—boiled flesh—you saw bits of wood, pebbles, and pieces of broken porcelain, the color bleached out of it all by the boiling water.

"Miss," Officer Regis said, his voice pained and his whole body shaking, "where is your nephew?"

"I told you, he's dead and I killed him! He's in that pot!"

Officer Jamison reached for his radio and called out, "We need backup. We have a missing child and a possible EDP."

"Where did he go?" the camera swung back and forth as Auntie Lena searched frantically for whatever it was she had just boiled alive. "Do they just disappear after you burn them?"

"Miss, give me the camera."

Officer Regis reached his blistered hand, with its weeping sores, into view of the camera as he fought Auntie Lena for the device. She fought and screamed, and the camera shook and the audio cracked before it went crashing to the ground.

That's where the video cut out.

The next day, Auntie_lena314 was scrubbed from the host site. I'm sure the police would have been very interested to see what Auntie Lena had been documenting in the first few weeks of her nephew's life, but the host site certainly had good reason not to hand over those recordings which were, essentially, video evidence of a girl slowly going mad and them doing nothing to stop it. But with no actual video, witness statements were worthless.

It also did nothing to tell Auntie Lena's loyal viewers just what happened to her. But if you knew what to type into a search engine, you were still able to follow what happened to her. In rural New York, a fifteen-year-old Lena McCannon was arrested in connection with the disappearance of her nephew, Henry. She insisted she had killed the baby, boiling it alive, but was never able to produce a body. In a hearing, she was deemed incompetent to stand trial. She now resides in the same psychiatric hospital as her sister, Nan, until such time as she is deemed fit to proceed.

The Rockland county sheriff's office asks that anyone who has any information about the whereabouts of Henry McCannon to please contact them.

A Wonder Made of Skulls
Barry Charman

IT WASN'T CLEAR AT what point time travel became less about the destination and more about the journey.

Judd reread the line, expecting something to reveal itself, but it was just too glib. The brochure was so glossy it came with a migraine warning. He wanted to put it away, but he was trying to get into the mood.

That made him think. At what point had time travellers had to *get in the mood?*

They were trying to make you feel important when you were about to be dwarfed by your unimportance. It didn't work. He put the magazine away and closed his eyes, thinking about all the things it didn't tell you.

Someone had to go and break the speed of thought.

They'd *called* it a breakthrough, then gone on to break through whatever else they could find. There were straightforward advances to begin with, then the achievements became more and more radical. Even so, no one had expected to break through *time*. It was an inspired accident, an innovative mistake. But things tend to get out of control when they're not planned.

All too quickly, time had been unravelled. It was divided up, mapped and auctioned off, becoming a commodity, an amusement. *The past is a foreign country, they do things differently there*; and a time traveller's favourite past-time was to go walk in the past, pointing and laughing at *foreigners*. What was stated first as a philosophical observation quickly became an advertising legend.

This activity had kept Judd busy for ten thousand years. Well, ten thousand years had kept him busy for the best of one. His desk job had started to get claustrophobic when the small print began dancing. They'd told him to take a break, go off and take a time-out. He remembered how Leonard had slapped him on the back, told him to go "pick the Sphinx's nose."

He squeezed the pads implanted beneath his fingers, called up a time door, and walked though, careful as always to lock it behind him. He emerged back in the deep past.

Great. *The Dinobores.* Judd smiled thinly; the height of technology was the act of yawning at a dinosaur.

There was an old saying: *Don't close the brackets.* In travellers' parlance, this meant: be wary of excessive time travel. Don't go too far back or too far ahead. The mind might not accept what it sees. Keep the possibilities open, allow time to *breathe.* Judd had gone prehistoric before; he'd taken the tour to the mud pits, taken pictures as an ancestor had half drowned on dry land. *A confusing spectacle,* they called it. *Fifty credits! Get your picture taken by one of our official guides!*

What a waste.

He only came back because it reminded him of Becky. She'd loved being *scared,* would grab his arm then laugh at herself. Odd, the things one remembered.

There was nothing more desolate than a glimpse of man's raw beginnings. Few did the tour twice. Same for the future. Half of Europe is a road of skulls, and no one wants to know why. A vision you can't change is a terrible thing.

Judd walked over to a rock and sat; he watched a Diplodocus as it walked in the distance towards some trees. He instinctively lifted a finger to the side of his head. One tap would activate the camera attached to his cornea. A nice picture for the folks back home. Subtle. Non-intrusive. Dull.

He lowered the hand, then turned to look back at his footprints. Walking backwards, they stopped abruptly with no indication to their origin. The door was gone for now, waiting to be called.

Judd sighed. Somewhere, he'd lost the magic. He remembered his first tour, that tight panic he'd felt when he'd turned and saw the door gone.

He got up and took a walk, wondering *when* he could go from here.

Rome? There was a great tour he'd heard about. He could toast marshmallows in the fire as the city burnt. They made it *fun.* He'd heard about their last tour, where they'd had a contest seeing who could tickle Schopenhauer first.

Mind you, it *was* getting a bit reckless. It had all been so solemn once, almost anxiously over-regulated. But slowly, over time, the tours had become more flexible. Of course, there were always some people saying they were on the verge of vandalism. But if you didn't make history interactive, then what was it? A pantomime parade of the dead.

The politicians had nightmares at first—about governments undoing each other and rewriting history—but the regulations had been strict enough to convince everyone. Even the religions had backed it up.

Create the doors, they'd said, *go through.*

He wondered what it was they'd expected to find. Had they given their endorsement expecting to find endorsement in turn? In the stirring of the past? If so, they hadn't got lucky. Faith hadn't endured time travel; it hadn't survived the *revelation.*

Judd had gotten a few laughs out of that. He'd replayed over and over the holo-discs of the priests who'd gone on one of the early tours; loving the looks of disappointment on their faces when they returned. Turned out religion had raised questions science could permanently answer. They'd always felt *special,* with the imaginary voice in their heads filling them up with hollow justifications for their every sin. Now, they were the same as everyone else.

Even now, Judd took some satisfaction at the memory. No one had ever made *him* feel special. His parents had preferred divorce over keeping the family together; mum had taken his brother but not *him.* She'd established a pattern. There should have been a girl waiting for him back home, but she'd moved on to someone else. The last time he'd seen her she'd dyed her silver hair blond, told him she was going off to marry someone in Paris in 1945. They'd picked out a nice spot, just after the war. They were going to set up a tasteless vineyard called *Hope's Fruit.* Hell, even his promotion had found someone else—

Judd paused and released a heavy sigh. He needed to remember why he'd taken this time off. His life had been closing in around him—constricting him, overwhelming him with the sheer banality of existing.

Tired, he called up a door.

Judd walked through, locked it, then looked around. He was on the *Marie Celeste*; they ran a neat tour. Usually threw a good boat party, at least.

The boat was deserted.

That's weird, he thought.

Wandering around the deck, Judd looked inside the cabins and down in the bunks. No one. There was always *someone* on the *Marie Celeste*.

There were just sounds that creaked in the wind and shadows that danced with the dust.

As the sun went down, Judd summoned another door and walked though.

Ah, Jerusalem. It always amused him that the Bible had evolved into just another brochure. Walking towards a narrow, winding road, he listened to the sounds of a distant market. It was dusk, and the sun here was also setting. The evening was mild, a soft breeze made him feel welcome.

There was a creak behind him.

Judd turned, frowning. The door was open. It should have disappeared as soon as he'd locked it—

Oh.

He winced. That was careless. If anyone had *seen...*

He walked back to the door and locked it. It vanished like a promise made in a dream.

As Judd was about to walk on, he looked down at his footprints.

Two pairs.

He remembered where he was and smiled wryly. Even so, the image was unsettling. He thought back to the *Marie Celeste*.

They had to lock the doors. Not just to keep the time periods sealed off, not just because you didn't want "foreigners" crossing the borders (which in itself was a parody of any period you visited), but also because of the *unknown*.

The *"what if"* as they called it back home.

What if there was something between the doors? And what if they forgot to *lock* the doors, and what if that something *noticed*...

Nonsense. The unnerved thoughts of people cowed by progress.

Still. They had broken the speed of thought, which *had* enabled them to open doors onto all of time and step through. You had to treat this stuff with some respect. He briefly thought of all the scare stories their scientists had flagged up. He'd only skimmed them, personally. It had all seemed so alarmist, so *feeble*.

They'd talked like time was a thread you could pull apart at any second. Before his first tour, there'd been a brief lecture on *unimaginable perversions*. That had been a popular phrase of theirs. Like they couldn't even predict how things could get messed up. Great bit of science, that.

Judd stared at the prints a little longer, then tried to shake off the feeling that was beginning to shadow him.

He checked his guide for the nearest meeting point, then activated his projector. Immediately, his clothing shimmered and he was disguised in the local attire. *Always blend in,* he thought, *and always lock your doors.*

Hurrying now, he made his way to the tour point: an innocuous grid reference that should have been bustling with tourists, each of them shimmering with an aura only an enhanced eye could detect. But there was no one there. He gazed around, expecting some tech to start giving him signals, but nothing happened. Just as Judd began to wonder what had happened to everyone, a door opened nearby. Surprised by how relieved he felt, he waited for someone to step through.

He waited.

When no one emerged, he approached the door, suddenly nervous. Everything beyond was dark. That meant nothing; it was a door, after all, not a window. Judd wanted to step through; even if it didn't take him home, he might come across a tour group. But why had no one appeared? Why had they left the way open like this?

What if he went through, and home had…altered?

Judd shut down those thoughts, appalled. He closed the door, and it vanished. Increasingly agitated, he ran into the humid night, checking his guide for the next tour point. Despite himself, he began to worry. The rumours began running through his mind again. The theories. They had made doors out of air. They had unwound the unknown. They had opened themselves up to new ideas, new possibilities.

What if they… had *become* doors?

What would that even mean? All of a sudden, Judd wanted nothing more than to be back behind his desk. Sure, life was small, trivial, but what the hell was the opposite? He shouldn't be here, scurrying about in some dim corner of the dark ages. His office was bland and dull and safe; he could feel it smirking at him from across time.

Something knocked. Someone answered.

That thought was wild, yet startlingly clear. As they had broken, could they *be* broken? What did that *mean*?

He saw a key in a lock, imagined entrance as a transference, a corruption, but had no means to shape or complete these thoughts. Stumbling as he went, he thought of that road of skulls and wondered where the first was laid, or the last.

"A mind is a terrible thing to taste..."

Judd stopped in the street. He shivered, feeling totally abandoned and adrift. In the silence, a distant animal howled. The wind coiled and moaned.

"Corrupted. Blind. Witless. Corruption follows. We are crawling over the back of time."

He tried not to panic. Just keep moving, he thought, on to the next door, and the next, and the next—

"Early, this. Malleable. Weapons will be made here. Prophets. Words will become mutilations."

Something was curling around his mind. An intimate sensation, wrong, unnatural. Judd felt disoriented. Suddenly, he remembered those early lectures, about *unimaginable perversions,* and all the rest. *Time travel is a wonder made of skulls.* That was a phrase he'd forgotten 'til now.

"Yes. Yes, it is."

He reached for a concept that he was unable to entirely grasp. Some fear thrown away in one debate or another, that science and religion could both be tools, one used to create the other, both used as fuel to tear everything else apart—

"We will begin here. Poor boy. So sad. So alone..."

Judd hurried into the night, followed closely by two pairs of footprints, the pervading sense of thoughtlessness that he'd brought with him, and a low voice that had begun to fester in his shadow.

A voice that told him he was *special.*

Masks

Jason LaVelle

THE ARTIST LOOKED DOWN at the subject, very pleased with what they had to work with. Though still and pale, the man's face had lost none of the appeal it held in life. A handsome face with hard jaw lines, a straight, prominent nose, and a smooth, not too long, not too shallow brow. The face was easily recognizable, a famous man especially in literary circles, one of the great fiction authors of the last decade. That was one thing death could never take from him: his achievements. And, of course, it could not take his face.

The artist began at his forehead, smearing thick alginate over the face, coating it gently but thoroughly, taking extra care to massage the thick white paste down into the hollows of his eyes so as to lose no detail. The artist's hands moved quickly, scooping more paste then smoothing it, thickening the coat and leaving only two small holes where the nostrils had been. With the man covered from hairline to chin, the artist massaged over the gooey paste once more, feeling and dispelling tiny air bubbles locked within. The alginate set quickly, only three minutes after mixing, and the artist hurried to place thin strips of burlap over the lumpy mask, strengthening the gelatinous mold.

A stack of six-inch strips of plaster bandages lay next to the body, and the artist, using hands clad with blue nitrile, dipped the strips in warm water, squeezed them out, and layered the bandages over the hardening alginate. After placing the last piece of plaster bandage in a bowtie shape connecting the bridge of the nose to the lips, the artist stepped back, admiring the work.

Better. The artist nodded triumphantly. Each mold formed faster, more easily, and with greater detail. *Perfect.* The plaster wouldn't be ready to work with for another thirty minutes, which left time for the artist to clean up the actual scene of the crime.

Jessica set the newspaper down on her kitchen counter, but the face of Ernie Stalward stared up at her. She spooned oatmeal into her mouth, wincing as she caught a spoonful that didn't have sugar on it.

Body Found in Lake Macatawa; Renowned Author Ernie Stalward Dead.

She touched the paper, rubbing her fingers across the newsprint until they came away black. It was a wonder they still made these things, and more of a wonder that she subscribed to it. She lifted her fingers to her nose and drew in a gentle breath, savoring the smell of newsprint and paper.

She'd always preferred the printed word, and in a world of tablets and computers, that made her an oddity, a minority even. Jess let out a sigh and scraped the last of her oatmeal from the bowl. She wasn't shocked by the headline, but it gave her a chill just the same. Stalward was one of five notable authors recently killed in a series of murders that was absolutely astounding the press and media. "Serial Novelists Killed by Serial Killer," the headlines read, or things along those lines.

Jessica remembered the first death well, and the headline accompanying it. "Horror Aficionado Daniel A. Smith Killed by His Obsession." It was a ridiculous headline, in her opinion.

Smith had been killed and his body left in the deep north woods of New York, eviscerated and propped up against a tree. The search party reported that coyotes had eaten most of his 'fleshy' parts. There was no evidence that he knew his attacker, nor that his publishing business had anything to do with his death, but his fondness for the terrible and macabre encouraged the papers make colorful headlines that would have, in other circumstances, been laughed at. Ridiculous though they may be, it gave Jessica an eerie feeling, looking at the names of people she knew in such context.

Jess opened her daytime planner and flipped to the last pages. *Ernie Stalward, Interview* was written in red on last Wednesday's spot. Jess had been so happy to hear Stalward was taking interviews once again. For a freelance journalist, he was a big score.

Stalward had recently released "Doctor Love," a crime drama centered around a philanthropic doctor whose family and friends had no idea he was also using and murdering prostitutes. *A modern day Jack The Ripper* was how Jess had described it in her article. The piece was good; Stalward had been open and funny, even revealing, giving her readers a chance to see beyond the multimillionaire author and look at the mind of a man who had created great fiction.

The article hadn't even been printed when the police found Stalward's body, but Jess suspected this may expedite the process. "Ernie Stalward's Final Review," is what they would call it, or something like that. She leaned back against her barstool. She supposed it was a nice note to go out on, that interview; she'd been quite complementary. Jess tapped her fingers on the countertops. In the last six months, she had interviewed each of the authors who turned up dead. *I'm going to get a reputation for this. Almost like a priest,* she thought, *hearing their last confessions before they met their ends.*

The artist broke away the plaster mold, peeling it bit by brittle bit from the casting. When the alginate finally released, the mold broke free and the plaster *thunked* onto the table. The artist picked it up, holding the oval shaped stone and admiring it: Ernie Stalward's face, cast perfectly in light-grey gypsum. It was beautiful, the most successful death mask yet.

Using a fine dental pick, the artist gently skimmed the stone's surface, smoothing out tiny imperfections around the eyebrows and chipping away the excess plaster from Stalward's nostrils. The artist made one final pass with only gloved fingers, relying on touch to find any hidden burs. There were none. The face was a mask of perfection; perfection cast in stone.

"So beautiful," the artist breathed, holding Stalward's face close to their own. For a moment, the artist swayed on shaky legs, and tears fell from their face.

"Deep breaths," the artist said and gently replaced the mask on the table. Once the tremble settled out of the artist's hands, they came to rest on Stalward's face again, gently massaging the cheeks, then the bridge of the nose.

On the back of the mask, sunk into the plaster, was a thick wall anchor. The artist wiggled the anchor, making sure it was secure and that no cracks would appear, then brought the mask into the study. A sacred air, no less so than that of a church, filled the artist's study. Books and paintings adorned every surface in the room, but the real prizes hung on the wall above the antique hemlock desk. Four exquisite stone masks stared out into eternity, their noble features preserved in perfect detail with a stone plaster. In this room, the legends lived; in this place, they were immortals.

Ernie Stalward's face took its place on the wall next to Artie Cabrera, whose long, soft visage and slightly opened mouth reminded the artist of the monoliths on Easter Island. Compared to Artie, a loud, boastful science-fiction author, Stalward's face was refined, sophisticated, and spoke of a completely different personality. His features were those of an athlete-intellect, a man who, while writing the most gripping crime dramas of their lifetime had also become a para-Olympic triathlete, using his one leg not as a crutch, but as a platform to elevate all those who had been born differently. Ernie Stalward, a great man, now forever a part of this room and its famous inhabitants. The heaviness of the space grew overwhelming, and the artist was forced to retreat, promising the faces a swift return. All things had to be taken in turn and with patience.

The budget was stretched thin, and her publisher was already incensed by the rising cost of airline fuel, but in the end the promise of the interview won them over.

Jessica's contact inside the New Queensland Literary group had leaked to her that Sean Brandis was in the United States. The reclusive Brandis, hailing from the great Down Under, never toured, never interviewed, never appeared in the media in any fashion. In fact, it had been rumored that even the photo on his book jackets was fake.

"Dark Meat"—his epic tale of one aboriginal's journey through life in a racist and separatist Australia to find peace and meaning in a culture that had been raped and dismantled by white colonist—was hailed as the greatest piece of Australian literary fiction in the past century. He was a treasure amongst aussies, even though his book was a scathing reprisal to the mostly white continent. "The Australian Herman Hesse," they called him. And he was here.

Jessica had been on her email and her phone all morning, checking, confirming, then rechecking. It was true. Her very last call was to the owner of the Air B&B condo Brandis had rented in Panama City beach. Only after she promised cash and internet notoriety did they divulge that he was indeed hosting Brandis in his house.

"This is it," she told the magazine, "the biggest interview of my life, and probably the best article you'll ever get."

Well, things like that never went over well. *Literary Face* had been in business for many years and had employed not only dozens of talented journalists, but they'd published articles on the biggest authors and screenwriters in the world.

"None like this though," Jess had argued. "This is going to be like unmasking Daft Punk or revealing the true creator of the Bible."

Okay, so maybe she was being a little overdramatic, but she wanted this. Bad. Five years of writing non-fiction articles and the occasional short story had left her with solid freelancing credentials and a reputation for being straight to the point but elegant in a way non-fiction almost never was. "Jessica Perth, the Joan Didion of our generation," she liked to fantasize.

So, stumbling out of the shower naked and dripping all over her tile floor, Jessica leapt for the phone on her counter to see the message thumbnail: *Flight Booked, make it good.*

"Yes!" she screamed, then slipped and cracked her ass on the hard tile in her kitchen. Goddam if this wasn't undignified, naked in a pool of still soapy water. Who knew where her phone flew off to when she fell, probably under the stove. She didn't care. She'd done it; she was going to meet the man with no face.

Florida had been napping quietly under a blanket of humidity when Jessica arrived. At 5:30 p.m., and by the time she tucked her suitcase in the trunk and buckled into her rental car, she was already soaked in perspiration. A Midwesterner by birth, humidity was not an unknown, but the thickness of it took her breath away. Each step felt heavy, and her clothes clung to her uncomfortably. Her toes, tucked neatly into thirty-dollar flats, were slimy and hot.

As she drove, Jessica mentally prepared for her assault on the Australian author. It would be a surprise attack, no warning, and that was usually the best kind. However, she'd had more than one door slammed in her face, and she couldn't let that happen today. That was the sticking part, getting in the door. Once she had Brandis in front of her, Jessica knew she could deliver the interview of a lifetime. But she had to get in.

Waterfront condos flew by outside her window. In the gaps between buildings, Jessica could see the ocean, sparkling and blue-green, an endless expanse of water extending far beyond the horizon. The GPS alerted her, and Jessica looked ahead 500 feet, where a two-story condominium building with grey sides and blue trim rested quietly off the road, watching the water. *Unassuming,* she thought. *Very smart.*

The driveway held a Range Rover and a bright blue moped. The garage door was down and the drapes were drawn. Jessica frowned as she slowed outside the building. Then she cleared the side of another structure and saw the tall fence behind the condo. She slowed further. A swimming pool with people in it.

A loud screech sounded behind her, and the blaring of a horn. Jessica looked into the rearview mirror just moments before a red pickup truck overtook her. She jammed on the gas and braced for impact, jerking the wheel as she did. Her tiny rental squawked and jumped the curb, leapt over a small patch of dry grass, and ground to a stop off the road. Her heart thudded loudly in her ears. Her hands trembled and she flipped the shifter up into park. Then she hugged her chest, rocking gently against her seat as her vision swam and surfaced then dove once more.

Then her door was yanked open. Jessica jumped back in her seat, wide eyed.

"What the fuck is your problem?" A bald man with a red face and a light blue polo top leaned into the car, jamming his finger in her direction.

Jessica couldn't respond, couldn't think. In fact, she could hardly breathe.

"You dumb bitch, you almost fucked up my truck! What the fuck were you stopped in the middle of the road for, you dumbass?"

"I—I, uh," as a writer, she'd never run out of words, until now.

"Get your ass out here, you stupid bitch! Are you drunk or something? Get out here!" The man reached in for her. Sweat dripped off his long nose onto her pants.

"Ey!"

The man looked up as another male voice shouted over to them. Jessica saw the man approaching through the windshield. He walked with a calm swagger, each step a little exaggerated, and though his limbs moved slowly, the man covered ground quickly. A Caucasian male, his thick brown hair was wet and matted on his head. He had a full beard, a mess of riotous curls that dripped off his cheeks and down his neck. His chest was bare and pink with sun exposure. He wore board shorts that stopped at his knees, shorts adorned with blue dolphins jumping through teal waves.

"Whacha doin' there, mate?" the man called. Though he wasn't shouting, his voice carried easily.

Her would-be attacker withdrew from her car and rose to meet the newcomer.

"This bitch nearly ran me off the road."

"How 'bout you cool down a bit, eh?"

"Why don't you go back to where you came from, moron! This isn't your business!"

The man came to stand right next to the car, only a yard away from the red-faced man with the pickup truck.

"I'm afraid that it is. See, she crash-landed here in my driveway, so the way I see it, is she's my responsibility now."

Jessica looked around and saw she'd landed right in the lot she had been stalking; her car had come to a stop only inches away from the little blue moped. *Holy shit*, she thought. *This is him. This is Brandis.*

"Your responsibility? Then you want to take responsibility for what she's done? To my truck?" The red-faced man was somehow turning more red.

Brandis looked around and spotted the truck. "Your truck looks fine to me, mate. Why don't you just drop it?"

The man huffed. "I took about an inch off my new tires trying not to hit her. Now who's going to pay for that?"

Brandis nodded, his beard dancing in a hypnotic way in the hot breeze.

"So, your tires and brakes did what they were supposed to do, right? That's their job, to stop you in case of an accident? Well, then good on them. The way I see it, you should walk away just happy you got them new tires on in time to save your big ass."

The man didn't know how to respond, so he did what all angry men do. He extended a finger and jabbed it at Brandis. The bearded man, who was neither large nor muscular, caught the man's hand and twisted inward. Jessica flinched as suddenly the red-faced man was on his knees in front of Brandis. Brandis spoke in a lower voice, but maintained his cool demeanor.

Jessica strained to hear.

"Now, you can take those new tires and shove them right up your bloody cunt. You stop acting like a prissy bitch and get your fat ass outta here right now before I break your jimmy-yanker. You understand that, mate?"

There was a tense stalemate. Well, tense for the red-faced man. Brandis looked as calm as he had when he'd first strolled into the situation.

"What's that mate?" he asked.

The man mumbled something and Brandis released him. The red-faced man looked over to Jessica once more before shaking his head and walking away, rubbing his wrist as he did so. Brandis watched him go, then came around to her door and peeked inside.

"You all right in there, miss?"

Jessica nodded. Though it was carpeted in thick brown beard, his face was kind and his hazel eyes glimmered from under thick eyebrows.

"You wanna come out? Have a glass of water? Or a beer?"

She hesitated. Here she was, exactly where she wanted to be. *Suck it up and go!* her mind shouted at her. Jessica nodded. "Yeah, that would be nice."

She accepted Brandis's hand when he extended it to her. The ground was shaky beneath her, and she wobbled a little.

"Hey there, easy does it," Brandis said, looping an arm around her. "Let me walk with you, all right?"

"Okay," she mumbled. She let Brandis lead her to the condo and in through the front door.

The house was nicely furnished but poorly lit, giving the space a moody appearance. The brightest light in the place shone in through the slider off the dining room, where the afternoon sun made its slow dance toward the ocean.

"Nice place," she said.

"Thanks, love. It's just a rental, though. I'm from out of town," he said, then gave a chuckle, as if it wasn't obvious he wasn't from there—his accent was unmistakable.

"Here," he said, motioning to a tan microfiber sofa. "Rest your feet for a minute and I'll get you a drink."

The artist packed the suitcase. The case was a hard-sided Samsonite, and not cheap, but good quality items rarely are. Certain necessities went in first: a white smock, blue scrub pants, two-dozen rubber gloves. Three plastic mixing spatulas went in, and a yard of folded burlap. The case still had plenty of room. The artist eyeballed a bag of alginate powder, the paste-like mix which was applied to the subject first that would capture the fine details of their face. *It should be plenty,* the artist decided and carefully set it in the suitcase, then added a long stack of plaster bandages wrapped in cellophane. The last item was a ten-pound bag of ultra-cal 30, the plaster powder that would make up the meat of the death mask. As an afterthought, the artist threw in a change of socks and underwear, along with a short, ironwood dowel with a length of heavy cord. A well-practiced routine, but even still the artist had to work to keep calm and be thorough. The prospect of a new subject always invigorated them, but vigor invited mistakes, and the precise nature of the art was most important. Some say that art imitates life, and some the opposite, but in this case, and not so humbly, the artist felt that their work created not only life but immortality.

"So, you're an artist then?" Jessica asked, her feet curled beneath her on the sofa and a tall glass bottle of beer in her hands.

Brandis laid a towel out on the loveseat opposite her and sat down. His belly pooched out slightly as he sat. He punched at his phone several times then set it on the couch next to him.

"I guess you could say that," he said, and pulled on his beer. "I write books."

Jessica nodded. "That's cool, anything I might know?"

"Well, do you read?"

"I do."

"Then you might know it."

Jessica sighed and rolled her eyes. "Come on, spill it. What do you write?"

"Have you heard of 'Dark Meat'?"

Jessica waited for what she hoped was an appropriate amount of time, then widened her eyes. "You're kidding! You wrote 'Dark Meat'? I love that book!"

Brandis raised his eyebrows at her and pulled on the beer again.

"Wow, I can't believe that's you. Didn't that book win a bunch of awards?"

Brandis shrugged. "Shite, if you ask me. I was in college when I wrote it, bored with class, so I did it to entertain myself. It was all bullshit, though, just fiction."

Jessica shook her head. "How can you call it bullshit? 'Dark Meat' was incredible, and so influential. It changed the way I thought about Australia."

"Eh. It was only incredible and everything because most people don't know shite about Australia. I mean, no offense miss, but do you know anything about Australia besides what was in that book?"

"I guess not. I used to watch The Crocodile Hunter a lot."

Brandis laughed so hard, he spat foam down his beard."

"The Crocodile Hunter? Oh, come on! Ha! But that's what I'm talking about. Nobody knows what really happens out back, so none of you know if the book was total shite or not."

Jessica thought about that for a minute while she drank. This interview was not going the way she planned—it was even better.

"So how do you explain all the awards, the success? Don't you think that if the book was shit that people would have called you out on it?"

"See, that's the funny thing about people, isn't it? They move in herds, just like cattle. A few people start talking about something they like, and pretty soon everyone else jumps on board with 'em." Brandis leaned forward so that the light of the room shone into his eyes. He looked…intense. "I wrote a story about a boy who had a shit life and was always trying to figure out what the hell he was supposed to do."

"No, it was way more than that, it wasn't just about a boy. It was about an entire culture, one that was ransacked. You're undervaluing the book now."

Brandis leaned back and shook his head. "You want me to tell you a secret about that book?"

Oh god yes!

"Yeah, sure."

"Well, when I first wrote it, the story was about me."

Jessica had to fight to keep her jaw from dropping as she stared at the man.

"The story about the dark-skinned aboriginal boy fighting his way through a tormented life was about you?"

Brandis smirked. "Yes ma'am. I only made him an aboriginal when my writing proff told me the story lacked any societal value. I figured the aboriginal angle would make it more—sympathetic, I guess."

Holy shit.

"That's our secret, though, got it?" Brandis said. "I get you out of your car trouble and you keep my secret. Fair enough?"

Jessica nodded. *Gold. Pure gold.*

"Wow, I feel like you've just blown my mind." Jessica's body was practically humming with excitement. And need.

"It's funny meeting you like this, you having read my book and all," Brandis said. His face was round beneath his beard, and a new curiosity crept into his eyes. "So, what brought you to Florida anyway? How did you end up in my driveway?"

Uh-oh.

A knock on the door saved her.

Jessica startled and stood.

"No worries, love, that's just my mate, Jon."

"Jon—"

"Yeah, you'll love him, he's a writer too."

Jessica bristled with that feeling, that strange lust, that uncertain something between excitement and need.

Brandis whipped open the door and was nearly flattened by a man who seemed impossibly large. The man caught Brandis with both arms and the Australian author was swallowed by his hug, disappearing for a moment behind the man's hairy arms.

"Christ, Phrater, you daft cunt, did you manage to get bigger?" Brandis gasped from within the man's grip.

Brandis was released and the big man slapped him on the bicep. "If you weren't such a little pussy, you could take it! Aren't you eating at all out there?"

Then the pair seemed to notice Jessica at the same time and stared in her direction.

Jess raised her eyebrows at them.

"Quite the bromance you've got there," she said. "So, is this an author thing, or are you guys just a little hot for each other?"

Brandis laughed, and she could swear the laughter came out with a thick Australian accent.

"Jon Phrater, this is Jessica—I'm sorry, love, I don't know your last name."

She rose to meet the big man. "I'm Jessica Perth," she said, and extended her hand.

Jon grinned at her, a grin that turned into a wide, large-toothed smile. His hand engulfed hers. "I'm pleased to meet you, Jessica." He spoke with a New York accent and pumped her hand twice.

Jon looked back at Brandis. "Where did you find her?"

Brandis eyed her curiously again. "Well, she just kinda got dumped into my lap. But I'm not sorry she did."

Jon still held her hand. The big man was hot and a little sweaty, and Jess felt her own hand beginning to perspire as well.

"Good find, Sean, good find." Jon finally released her hand.

"I hear you're a writer too?" Jess said.

"You've been telling stories, eh, Sean?"

Brandis chuckled. "Come on, let's have a beer."

"Let's do that, but I want to sit next to Miss Perth."

"Jesus, you're creeping her out, you fat American idiot."

"Oh come on, you sound like the spawn of a hillbilly and a British whore. I If anybody's creeping her out, it's you."

Jon was still staring at her, still smiling. He had a strange light in his eyes, a glimmer—no, more like a shimmer, like the shine of a river in the moonlight, slippery, smooth, never-ending.

Deep breaths, Jess, deep breaths. Sean Effing Brandis, and Jon—Prince of Sci-Fi—Phrater. This trip had gone from gold to platinum.

"Boys, nobody is creeping me out, but I need you to excuse me for a minute. I want to go grab something out of my bag in the car."

Jon faltered, and Brandis gave her a look that clearly said no.

"I promise, I'll be right back."

Jon looked to Brandis and the bearded man gave a thin tip of his head. Phrater sighed and made an obvious attempt to freshen his smile.

Jessica shook as she opened the trunk of her rental. She grabbed the handle of her large suitcase, started to lift, then dropped it back into the trunk-well. She reached for the trunk again, and her slender hands shook so fast in the Florida heat that they looked like a mirage.

"Come on, honey, you've got this," she whispered. The biggest opportunity in her life lay before her, and here she stood, shaking like a frightened fifteen-year-old before her first school dance. *I had every reason to be frightened, and look how that dance turned out.* Jessica blew out a deep breath and snapped open the suitcase. She rummaged through the contents for a moment, slipped several items into her pockets, then finally withdrew from the trunk.

The two men were waiting for her in the living room, and they both visibly relaxed when she stepped back through the door. Jessica smiled as she walked into the room.

"You're in my spot," she said, approaching Jon.

The large man smiled wide again and patted his leg.

"Why don't you come sit on Papa Jon's lap?"

Brandis rolled his eyes, but smirked.

"Are you supposed to be Santa Claus now, in the off-season?" Jess asked. One hand slipped into her pocket and started fiddling with the things from her bag.

Jon's laugh was deep and meaty, then he slid over, allowing about twelve inches on the cushion next to him.

Jessica squeezed into the spot then grabbed her beer off the end table next to her and drained the last of it. That steady energy was rising in her again. Anticipation, excitement, desire.

Brandis shifted around in his seat.

"So, you ever got to talk to a famous author before?" Jon asked, leaning too close to her.

"Can't say I have," Jessica answered, glancing over at Jon then looking down into her beer bottle.

"Pretty cool, isn't it?"

"I suppose. You're *friendlier* than I would have thought."

"You've heard of me then?" Jon asked.

"Well, I've heard of *him*," Jessica answered, motioning to Brandis, who burst out laughing.

She looked back at Jon, who was still staring at her. His smile had faded into a grin, but there wasn't any mirth in it.

Jon was breathing heavily, and she got the impression that he was trying to smell her. Jon Phrater, she determined, was a bit of a creep.

"I'm going to hit the pisser," Brandis said and left the room.

As soon as he disappeared down the hall, Phrater leaned closer.

Jessica leaned away, but the big man pulled her face toward him.

"It's okay to be nervous," he said, then put his mouth over hers.

Not the interview she had envisioned. Phrater obviously had one thing on his mind, and there was no getting through to men once they had *that* in their heads. The kiss was slimy and hot, and Jessica thought there could be no better time than this. She withdrew the cord from her pocket, and while Phrater explored her mouth, she looped the cord up and around his neck, then back down again. Phrater paused.

"What are you—"

Jessica gripped both ends of the cord, pulled her knees up to her chest, then kicked out against him with all her strength. Phrater's body jerked back but his head and neck snapped forward.

She reamed on the cord. His face turned red, spittle formed on his lips, and he tried and failed to sputter out some complaint. The cord burned her hands but Jessica pulled harder, pistoning out with her legs as she did. Phrater's eyes bulged from his head, and just when she thought they would burst right out of their sockets, she heard a muffled *crack* and his body went limp, falling on top of her.

Jessica desperately needed a minute to rest, but she didn't have time. She squeezed out from under Phrater's soft body and hurried down the hall after Brandis.

"Argh!" Jessica grunted as she tightened the garrote. Her hands ached from gripping the wooden bar, but she kept applying pressure. Brandis batted at her face, but his weak attempts couldn't hurt her now. He hadn't had any oxygen for over a minute and his carotid arteries were dissecting. Blood leaked from his nose as the vessels tore themselves open. The bearded author began to stroke and asphyxiate at the same time.

He was as good as gone, Jessica just had to wait for his body to realize it was dead.

Finally, Brandis gave up his struggle. His hands dropped away from his neck. His body shuddered then fell onto the floor, where a dark pool of urine bloomed beneath him.

Jessica sagged, drawing deep breaths with her hands on her knees. *Holy shit, what a workout!* Jon had been a relative pushover despite his size. But this Aussie, he'd been determined!

She wiped sweat, spit, and blood off her face and walked out of the condo to retrieve her suitcase from the car. No one watched her. That was good. She'd almost blown the whole damn thing a couple hours ago by not paying attention while she was driving. *My god, the tragedy that had almost become.* A shiver ran through her; she didn't even want to think about it.

The large Samsonite rolled smoothly over sealed asphalt and skipped up the steps and into the condo. Jessica locked herself in and opened the case in the living room, pulling out her casting supplies. It would be close, but she thought she might have just enough to do them both. She grabbed Brandis and rolled him over, bending down to examine his face. She pet his beard as she took in all of his defining features. The man with no face, hers at last, forever.

"Don't worry, love, your secret is safe with me."

Off-World Kick Murder Squad VI

Daniel Arthur Smith

This is the sixth episode of the serialized novel Off-World Kick Murder Squad. Earlier episodes can be read in the previous Canyons issues

AS THE *JENTU* FELL, the twilight horizon slipped from view and–for the second time in as many days–the fast approaching forest filled the windscreen. I'd managed to buckle into the jump seat, but that didn't diminish the sensation of my belly rushing up to my gut.

Thunderous blasts continued beyond the hull, bouncing the ship between a sandwich of concussions. Then the explosions stopped, leaving the bridge eerily quiet in their absence.

Anson cleared his throat, "*Hrrmm*," then softly said, "Well, at least they've stopped firing."

"They see us going down," said Bailer. "They know were dead in the air."

Anson wasn't fazed. "That's not exactly true."

I wasn't as calm. "What do you mean?"

"I mean we're okay," he said.

"The lights are out. The engines are out. We're falling out of the sky." I threw my hands up but right then, the cabin shook so hard I had to grab back down to the sides of my seat so as not to fall over. "From where I sit, I fail to see how we're okay."

"We will be in a minute," said Anson. "It's not an EMP."

"How do you know?" I asked.

He tugged at the yoke. "Because I still have a heavy stick. Let's just ease back…" Anson pulled back on the yoke and the horizon crept back into view. He reached his arm down by his side, and, with a *click*, a scarlet glow washed over the console. "That's better," he said. "Bailer buddy, how are you doing?"

"Fine," said Bailer.

"And you, Cap?"

"Swell," I said, and I was. "Glad you're the one flying the *Jentu*."

"I appreciate the vote of confidence," said Anson, then he gently tilted to the side. The *Jentu* followed, shifting her glide path toward the shadowed contours of the dark valley below. "I can go another klick or two before we have to set her down, but I'm confident we can reboot before that."

"What do we need to do?" I asked.

"You just sit tight, Cap. Bailer's got this. Those concussion blasts they were firing affected the airflow around the *Jentu* and caused the compressors to stall, which triggered a safety feature, disabling the power. We just need to turn those engine compressors back on."

"Put disabling that safety feature high on your list of things that need doing."

"It's kind of important," said Anson. "The way it's supposed to work—"

I cut him off, "Just put disabling that safety feature on your list."

"Yes, Cap. Bailer, grab that red lever. On three, I'll flip the one on my side and you flip yours. One...two...three."

Zwoosheeep! The console went as flashy as a casino table, stabilizing when all of the control indicators and screens were properly engaged.

"All right," said Anson. "Now to get to the river." He gently turned the yoke and the *Jentu* veered to port. "Okay. Switch off all four of the thruster engines, and when I give you the signal, you turn them all on again."

Bailer nodded. "Got it," he said, then flipped the four toggles down. "Ready on your mark."

What I noticed was the black of a mountainside coming in fast before us. "Anson," I said. "You do see we're running out of valley?"

"Just a second more, Cap."

By that point we were skimming the canopy, and the tallest of the trees began to brush against the underside of the delta wings, abruptly jostling the *Jentu* starboard to port and back. I can tell you, the jump seat was becoming mighty restrictive and with each bump I was getting a bit more uneasy.

"Any time would be good."

"Just a sec..."

"You keep saying that, but I don't know that we have a second more."

"And there it is," said Anson. "Hold on."

"There it is what?"

"The waterfall."

"Waterfall?" I asked.

"We're about to go over," said Anson. "Hold on tight. Bailer, get ready."

I wasn't ready. "Over a waterfall? Why do we have to go—"

Then the nose of the *Jentu* took a radical dive down and before my eyes, the shadowy top of the canopy beyond the windscreen disappeared to a wide opening of darkness then—the boiling white waters of the river below.

I white-knuckled the sides of my seat and pulled myself into it. "*Whooooaa,*" I yelled as the river rushed closer and my gut raced to my head.

Anson reached to the throttle quadrant of the helm and grabbed 'hold of the master lever. "Now!" he yelled.

Bailer threw all four of the switches up.

Zweeeee-EEEERRRRR! The thrusters ignited and Anson pushed the master lever forward.

RRRRR!

The engines roared loudly and the bridge quaked and shuddered so much, I had to clench my teeth from the rattle; then just like that, Anson pulled the *Jentu* from the dive, up toward the soft purple of the morning sky.

"We'll still have to set down to do diagnostics and repairs," he said.

"And to disable that safety feature," I added. "Nothing too safe about a stall while being pursued by anyone less than happy with us."

"Yes, Captain."

The foul odor that had permeated the bridge began to rapidly dissipate, filtered so quickly through the life support system, you wouldn't think the cabin had been smoke filled a moment before. I clicked off the safety buckle, freed myself of the jump seat, then hit the comm. "Is everyone all right down there?"

Cassidy answered. *"Anything that wasn't secured tight found a new place. Are we going to make a habit of this?"*

"I think not," I said. "I'll be down in a minute." I stepped between Anson and Bailor and placed a hand on their shoulders. "Great job, fellas."

They both responded with a cheery, "Thanks, Cap."

"Let's get a ways away before setting down. Bailer, you help him out."

Bailer said, "Sure thing." And Anson added, "It won't take long."

"Good," I said. "I want to get to sky sooner than later. If you need anything, let me know. I'm going down to help out the others and tend to our guest."

By the time I made it below, Cassidy, Rhia, and Rhoe were already picking up the pillows, clothes, and whatever else hadn't been secured. The only sign left of our near catastrophe was a bit of clutter strewn across the galley. My concern was our new guest and the reason for our mission: Cerulean Blue. So I went past the galley in the passenger dorm. There I found Hodge leaning against the wall outside of a spare cabin. He had his nose buried in a vid card. "Are you watching something from the Archive?" I asked.

"Alice in Wonderland," he said.

"I told you this place ain't like that."

He shrugged. "I know. But I like the story."

I peeked into the passenger cabin. Cerulean was seated on the end of the bunk at the far side of the room, rubbing his long, thin, scaled hands together above the heat vent.

"How's our guest?" I asked.

"Oh. He's fine," said Hodge. "Me? I've got the willies. It's those eyes. Just ain't right. Are you sure we're related to him?"

"Well. They say that the lizard men are the forerunners of the syn technology."

"Does that mean that syns, me and you and every other thing synthetic has a lizard brain?"

"No," I said. There may be more than some truth to that, but I didn't care to confuse Hodge any further. "He's from Indicus, the Blue Plane, and they're the founders of the technology. That's the only thing in common."

"Still gives me the willies."

I gave Hodge a nod and, without lifting his eyes from vid, he moved away from the door.

"Go help the girls," I said, "I'll want to chat with him for a bit."

"Okay," said Hodge. He couldn't have slipped past me any faster.

I stepped back to the door then, as my augments assessed the reptoid, I hesitated in a thought of my own. Cerulean had a foot on me at least, and at the end of those thin, bluish scaled hands were long, deep blue nails that could easily shred through me without much effort on his part, not to mention those dagger teeth. He could have taken any one of us out at his own choosing, which meant he'd chosen not to. But Hodge was right about those eyes. They were unsettling—or, I should say, those swirls of light where his eyes should be.

Now you might be thinking I'd be used to seeing eyes glow, living with syns and being a syn myself. But that isn't how it is. For the most part, the pupils of our eyes just happen to be a brighter color blue than most mortals, a cerulean blue that, in the right light, glows iridescent in the same way as a cat—if you ever saw a cat that wasn't a syn, I mean. Cats and most vertebrates have a layer just behind the retina called the tapetum lucidum, and it reflects the incoming light and thus increases night vision. Humans don't have that, unless they're Bureau Boys or modded like us.

That blue iridescent layer we have is due to the integration of organic, ocular, and neural tech—that tech being neural lace. The neural lace weaves through the brain, nervous system, and drapes right down behind our retinas, enhancing our vision and producing a glow—just like the layer of tapetum lucidum cats have. And it's the neural lace that links us back to Cerulean and his people.

A bit of history.

Like I said before, Cerulean is Indici, which means he's from the blue Indicus Plane. When the humans stumbled upon the Indici, they discovered that the ancient Indici technology was vastly superior to anything the humans had for themselves. At first, the Indici withheld their tech–hid it really–because they didn't like the humans. But then came the Battle of Uluru and the Spectral Wars, and that's when the Indici, albeit reluctantly, began to share—they hated humans, but they hated the invading Omni forces even more. The Indici were the ones who helped the Alpha Plane advance in crystal technology and, through organic synthetics, feed the homeland.

That's where we come in.

The first syns in the homeland were mechanical constructs. It was the Indici technology that led to organic synthetics. First hybrids, then fully programable organics—steel became bone. Organic synthetics are based on Indici physiology, programmed at creation with basic forms of neural lace. The neural lace is how our basic consciousness–the template for a soldier, a worker, a companion–is uploaded ready-made into our syn shells. That's how we're wide awake on day one, and leveraging that neural lace tech was our fall back plan for Will—if he was still in there.

We aren't the only ones to use it. The humans use neural lace too; they can also transfer conscience to syn shells and vice versa, like that time Cassidy transferred into that blood broker—but that's another story.

Nobody is quite sure how the Indici use the lace. Some say just to regenerate and that the lizard bodies aren't even their original form. Nobody in the Alpha Plane knows for sure. But my point is, at the end of the day, *we* have eyeballs but the eyes of Cerulean Blue were orbs of blue flame.

Now I could've entered into the conversation sternly. But I decided to show Cerulean some kindness. Reason being, like I said, he could have taken any one of us out and he'd chosen not to.

I rapped my knuckles on the door jamb. "Mind if I join you?"

"Pleassse do," said Cerulean Blue. "I'm enjoying the heat. It wasss ssso caw-old in that sssell."

"I imagine," I said. I took a seat in a chair in the corner across from him. "The *Jentu* tends to run hot. Usually a bit much for me. But it must be real nice for you. After being in that ice-box and all."

"The persssisssstance of caw-old causssesss an ache-uh. I'm already feeling ssso much better." His head spasmed again in that weird lizard way and he fixed a stare in my direction. "Thank you," he said. "For liberating me from thossse confinesss."

"It was my pleasure," I said.

"You and your caw-rew. You are sss'ynthetics. Are you…" He paused, but I understood what he was asking.

I raised a brow. "Are we humans in syn skins? No. We're pure syn."

The reptoid softly chuckled, "*Ka, ka, ka, ka.*" At least that's what I think he was doing. It put an easy smile on my face. "What isss your name, sss'yn?"

"Eller," I said. "At your service."

"Pleasssure to meet you, Ellahr."

"Likewise. Except I don't know your name."

"And yet you sssaved me."

"Well. The people who hired me gave me a code. They called you Cerulean Blue."

"How fasss'cinating. You may call me Sss'karo."

"Sss'karo," I said with a nod. "So, Sss'karo. Those people in the compound had you in a cell. I'm not going to lie, I'm not partial to any of the five syndicates, or humans in general. So it's my bet they just weren't being all that hospitable. Am I correct about that?"

"You are caw-rrect."

"I'd also like to think it's a safe bet that you're peaceful and I'm not going to have to keep you confined to this room?"

"You are again caw-orrect."

"All right then. You're free to move around our little ship. There's protein in the galley you can help yourself to. No one will give you issue, but I should let you know, it's not every day we have a guest from the Blue Plane. In fact, this is the first time any of us onboard have actually met an Indici."

"I undersss'tand. I will kaw-eep my profile low."

"That is much appreciated."

"You sss'erve me an honor with your trust."

"It will make it much easier if we all get along." I stood up. "I'm sure you noticed the engine stall?"

"I did."

"It's remedied, but we'll have to briefly set down to go over the ship, then we'll be on our way and off world before you know it."

I kept my face to him as I stepped back through the doorway—keeping as casual and calm as I could make it look. I was about to turn and leave when he stopped me.

"Captain Ell-ah," he said. "You mentioned that you were hired?"

I had and that was admittedly a slip on my part. I would've preferred to make the rendezvous to deliver Sss'karo without furthering that point of discussion.

"Yes," I said. "I did mention that. That we were hired, I mean. I told you I wasn't going to lie, and I won't. It's like this. We do jobs. We don't ask questions. Now, some people were concerned about your situation and asked us to spring you. So we did." I started to turn again, thinking to slip away before Sss'karo asked another question. But he did anyway.

"And I'm free to go?"

"We were asked to save you, then deliver you to their safety. So that's what we're doing."

"Do you trussst them?"

And there it was. "Like I said. We do jobs. We don't ask questions."

His slender tongue slithered. "Are you curiousss asss to why I was being held?"

"I am not," I said. Of course I was. But start asking too many questions and you'll hit upon some you might not like the answers to.

"I wasss betrayed, held against my will."

"Well, I figured that, judging by the steel bands that bound you to that chair."

"I am much older than I appear. I sssplit with my people of the plane that share your planet eons ago, and have sssince inhabited the Indicusss Plane of this world. I believe that the Sss'yndicate wantsss technology and that they abducted me eith-aw to gain insightsss into my counterpartsss, or they are operating under the auspicesss of thossse sss'ame allied Indici."

"I appreciate you sharing, and though either of those things may be, in part or in total, true, it's no concern of mine."

"Do the people you are taking me to really wish for my freedom or do they want what they think I possess for themssselves?"

"Again, not a concern of mine."

"It should be."

"And why is that?"

"Because what I know could mean your end."

With those parting words, I went back to the bridge.

Not everything that Sss'karo said was clear to me, other than him believing that what he knew was something dangerous. But just what that danger was, or whether he meant it would be a harm to all life in general or particularly syns, wasn't clear to me. I didn't take it as a threat. If he wanted us dead, we would be. My bet was that he was looking to sway me to his favor and away from the mission at hand. Yet even knowing that, I couldn't shake the feeling his words had left me with. I usually wouldn't let anything get under my skin, but there was something about Sss'karo, and it didn't take long for what he said to gnaw into me.

That is exactly why we don't ask questions.

No one ever says anything you truly want to hear. They start speaking and before long, something said burrows into your head and starts you to second guessing yourself.

Anyway, we spent the next few hours heading back the way we came, skimming the canopy to stay stealthy, and when we were satisfied we were far enough away, I told Anson to set her down. He found a forest glade nestled between a high ridge and a small lake, which was a bit of a bonus because it allowed us to cycle water while we were there.

First things first, we did an outside inspection while Anson and Bailer went through every system on the ship. There were a few things to tune up, but nothing that needed repair. The outside was fine too. There was some light scoring from the anti-air fire, but whatever they blew up alongside the ship left no mark.

When Hodge and I were done inspecting, we flushed the purifiers and refilled the water system and reserve tanks. He was heading back toward the shore to pull the hose when he set his sights on a blue plumed, two-legged lizard bird near the water's edge—easily a meter taller than a man.

"You know," he said to me, "that there lizard bird looks like a big old chicken."

"I suppose it does," I said.

"I like chicken. There's that place on Riley where they grill chicken over an open fire. It's synthetic, of course, but it sure does taste good."

"Yeah. I remember that place. That meat was delicious."

Hodge shifted his lower jaw side-to-side as if there was already something in his mouth. "You know," he said, "the way I figure, if he looks like chicken, he should taste like chicken."

"There's only one way to find out," I said. I took a step forward, drew my blaster, and let loose a shot at the lizard's crested head. *Pew.* The tall bird collapsed on the shore.

"Well, all right!" Hodge said as he headed over to the bird.

Cassidy watched from the open loading bay. "Wow," she said. "Fresh water and fresh food."

"I think everyone will be happy with a change in protein."

"Ya," she said. "Sounds great. You know how to cook that thing?"

"I figure Hodge is right," I said. "It's just a big chicken."

"Sure," she said. "Shame we don't have a big oven."

The two of us watched Hodge as he tugged and pulled on the legs of the beast, barely moving it from where it had dropped.

"Hmm," I said. "Looks like we're going to have to cut it up. Aren't we?"

"Looks like," said Cassidy. "I'll get a torch."

There was some effort involved, but we butchered up one of those legs for a roast and froze the rest in the food store. Rhia and Rhoe, being vegetarians, gathered their own treasure of some fresh leeks and plant edibles they found outside the ship and we settled down for a feast. We invited Sss'karo to join us, but he didn't, which was just as well. I wasn't sure what he'd think about the main course. It also freed me up to have an after dinner talk with the squad.

"All right," I said after the last of the food was cleared, "now that we've got our bellies full, I wanted to talk a bit about our next steps."

Hodge raised his glass. "Hear, hear," he said. "Let's get off this rock."

"That's the immediate plan," I said. "It was a little hairy this morning, but we accomplished what we set out to do and as a bonus, we took on fresh water, vegetables, and protein. We've also gone through the *Jentu* and she's good to go. So as soon as the sun sets, we'll head off world to the rendezvous and exchange Sss'karo and the device for the remainder of our fee."

"And where's that?" asked Hodge. "Are you planning on tapping that quant again?"

"No. No quant," I said.

"'Cuz I don't like that," he added.

"First off, it's not a quant, second, our rendezvous is a hop-skimp-jump over to the fourth planet—Mars."

"We're going to Mars?" asked Hodge.

"Yep. Anson charted a flight plan and we'll be there just short of two weeks."

"Two weeks?" said Bailer.

"I think two weeks is fine," said Hodge. "As long as we aren't using that quant device."

"Yeah," said Bailer. "I'm with Hodge. But why so long? The solar sail should take half that time."

"I don't want to draw too much attention, being so close to Earth and all."

"Ah, agreed. So if everything is ready, why wait until dark? Albeit, there's less chance of being sighted. But even if we were, we haven't detected anything that could catch us. Unless of course they have some cannons sprinkled across the planet."

"I'd rather slide out peaceful like," I said. "Especially with our cargo."

"Cargo?" asked Hodge. "What's so special about the Indici?"

"He doesn't mean the Indici," said Cassidy. "Do you, Cap?"

"You're right. I don't. Downing this land bird gave me an idea. Anson looked it up. Tell them what you found."

Anson lifted a digital pad from beside him, tapped it, and projected a 3D holo-image that resembled the lizard bird. "According to the Archive, what we found is an *ornithomimid* which, for those of you who have tried it, is a particularly tasty creature. Now, it's supposed to be extinct, and there ain't nothing exactly like it being farmed anywhere."

Cassidy chimed in. "So you want to haul a load of the birds to Mars."

"Exactly," I said. "Most of the new Mars settlements are agricultural, fresh in the new terraformed atmosphere. A creature like the ortho...orno—"

Anson corrected, "Ornithomimid."

"Ornithomimid," I repeated. "A creature like this would be welcome. I say it's a safe bet that if we load up the hold with as many of these as we can carry, we'll be able to turn them for a tidy profit."

"Right," said Bailer. "I get it, and we could use the credits. But how are we supposed to explain how it is that we came upon these dinosaurs?"

"We just tell the farmers that they're synthetic," said Hodge. "Just like the little chickens on Riley."

Everyone looked at Hodge.

"What?" he said.

"That's a great idea," said Cassidy.

"Well, yeah," said Hodge. "That's why I said it. For an extinct bird, it is delicious. I mean, the dinner was excellent. So much better than eating protein paste, and I'm sure the Martian folk will feel the same way."

I shot Hodge a wink. "That's what I was thinking."

"Too bad there was only one of them," he said. "And we ate it."

"Oh," said Cassidy. "There are plenty more out there. I was just outside gathering the laundry and there was a group grazing by the edge of the lake."

"You don't say," I said. "Let's go take a look."

And just like Cassidy said, there was a whole herd, or flock, of those lizard birds gathered together in threes and fours of like colors—scarlet reds, brilliant indigo blues, and some crested in gold.

"Let's go round them up," I said.

"Round them up?" asked Cassidy.

"Steer them into the ship. It will be easy."

Which is exactly what we did.

And it was surprisingly easy. We staked some line in a vee away from the loading bay then I went with Hodge, Bailer, and Cassidy to flank them and together, we walked them toward the ship. Not so fast as to upset them–they were easily agitated–just enough to keep them moving.

Once they were inside, we closed the lift gate, then gathered up some of the lake moss and grasses we'd seen them feeding on.

We'd finished loading the bay ahead of schedule with daylight to spare, so we decided to take of advantage and go. We were moments from leaving when Anson called me over the ship's comm. "Cap," he said, "you might want to take a look at this."

I went up to the bridge with Hodge by my side. Anson and Bailer were leaning over the console veering out into the clearing beyond the ship.

"What is it?" I asked. "What are you looking at?"

Bailer stepped aside to give me space. "Something's upset the lizards."

I leaned forward to see for myself. "I'll be," I said. Lizards as small as your hand were skittering on two legs over the ridge through the clearing right alongside more of those lizard birds, and more than a few other four-legged varieties every other size in between.

"They're spooked," said Hodge. "You think it's that big fella we ran into last night?"

"I don't know," I said. "Could be. Something's certainly stirred them up. Are we good to go?"

"That we are, Cap," said Anson.

"Then let's get to doing just that."

Anson resumed his startup routine, throwing switches, checking this and that. The lights and screens of the console came back to life. I turned to go back below.

"Cap," he said.

"What's that?"

"We might have a problem."

He tapped the radar scope. The small console screen was lit up with a wave of color-coded dots moving in our direction from just beyond the ridge.

"That's not good," I said.

"Aren't those just more lizards?" asked Hodge.

"Not in formation. Anson, let's go."

The red emergency light went to blinking and the *Jentu*'s klaxon sounded.

"We're marked," said Anson.

"Shut that thing off," I said, then leaned forward again to the windscreen. A field of red squares filled my augments, scattered across the column of troopers and half a dozen artillery mechs topping the ridge.

We weren't going anywhere.

ABOUT THE AUTHORS

Molly Thynes is a Mental Health Counselor by day, writer of assorted morbid things the rest of the time.

Barry Charman is a starving writer of oddball stories. Published in **Ambit, Popshot, The Alarmist, Bare Fiction Magazine** & **Firewords Quarterly**.

Jason LaVelle is an author, photographer, and podcaster from West Michigan. When he's not spending time with his beautiful wife and four children, LaVelle works at a veterinary clinic, helping animals of all kinds. With his two pugs, Dragon and Mr. Sparkles, his Chihuahua, Mari, and his annoying dachshund, Lady, LaVelle pretty much lives in a zoo. After he's done playing with the pugs and tucking the kids into bed, LaVelle ventures down into the basement, where his umbrella cockatoo, Bella whispers in his ear like a demonic muse, forcing him to explore the paranormal world inside his mind.

Jessica West (a.k.a. West1Jess) is currently pursuing a state of self-induced psychosis, also known as writing. In the past, she has worked for Wal-Mart, a lawyer, and a bank. Now if she could just get a couple years experience with the IRS and the NSA, world domination is in the bag.
Jess lives in Acadiana with three daughters still young enough to think she's cool and a husband who knows better but likes her anyway.

For news and updates visit west1jess.com

Daniel Arthur Smith is a USA Today bestselling author. His titles include *Spectral Shift, Hugh Howey Lives, The Cathari Treasure, The Somali Deception*, and a few other novels and short stories. He also curates the phenomenal short fiction series *Tales from the Canyons of the Damned* and *Frontiers of Speculative Fiction*.

He was raised in Michigan and graduated from Western Michigan University where he studied philosophy, with focus on cognitive science, meta-physics, and comparative religion. He began his career as a bartender, barista, poetry house proprietor, teacher, and then became a technologist and futurist for the Fortune 100 across the Americas and Europe.

Daniel has traveled to over 300 cities in 22 countries, residing in Los Angeles, Kalamazoo, Prague, Crete, and now writes in Manhattan where he lives with his wife and young sons.

For news and updates visit danielarthursmith.com